I LOVE
CHRISTMAS!

Copyright © 2007 by Hans Wilhelm, Inc.

All rights reserved. Published by Scholastic Inc.
SCHOLASTIC, CARTWHEEL BOOKS, NOODLES, and associated logos
are trademarks and/or registered trademarks of Scholastic Inc.
Lexile is a registered trademark of MetaMetrics, Inc.

Library of Congress Cataloging-in-Publication Data is available.

ISBN 978-0-545-27466-1

12 11 10 9 8 7 6 5 4 3 2 1   10 11 12 13 14 15/0

Printed in the U.S.A. 40 • This edition first printing, September 2010

noodles®

I LOVE CHRISTMAS!

SCHOLASTIC READER · LEVEL 1 · 50-250 WORDS

by Hans Wilhelm

Cartwheel
·B·O·O·K·S·®

SCHOLASTIC INC.
New York Toronto London Auckland
Sydney Mexico City New Delhi Hong Kong

It's Christmastime.
Everybody is so busy.

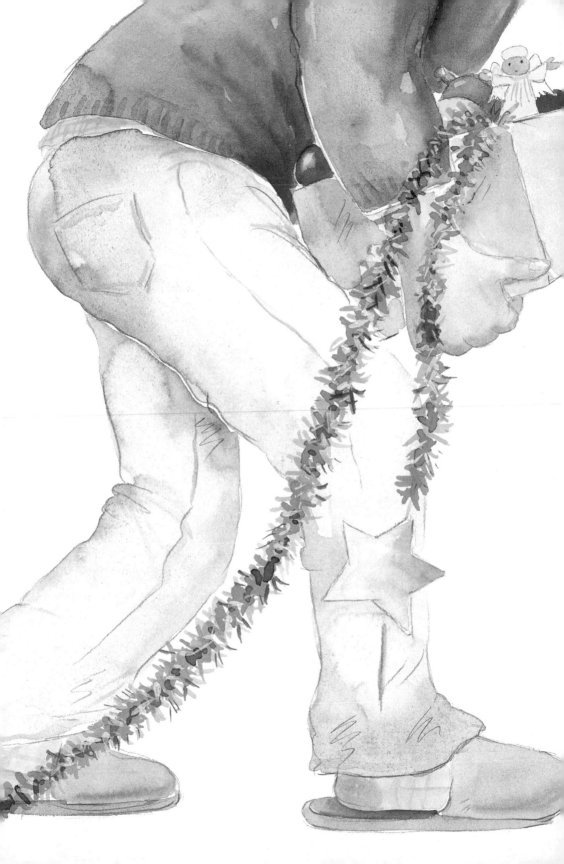

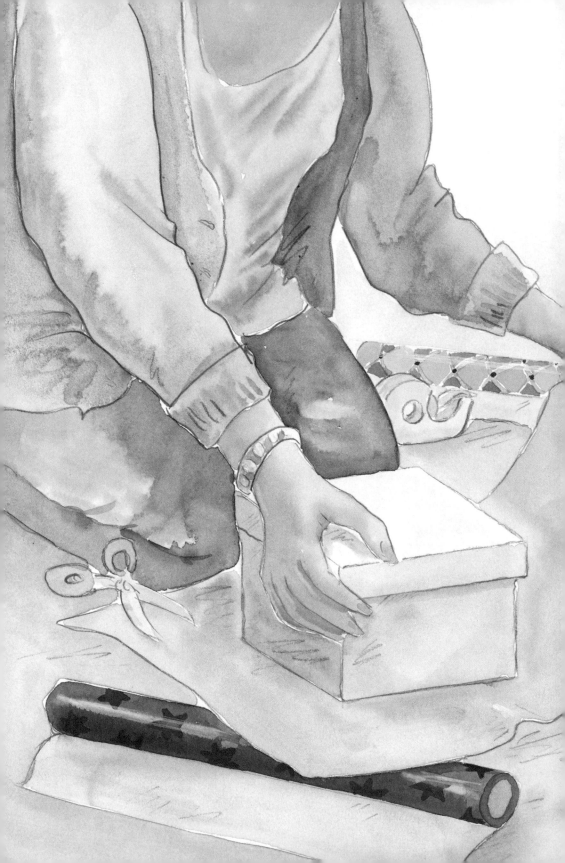

Can we go for a walk?

Can we play ball?

Can I have a snack?

No one has time for me.

I don't like Christmas!

Wait!
I know what I can do!

I can join
the Christmas fun.

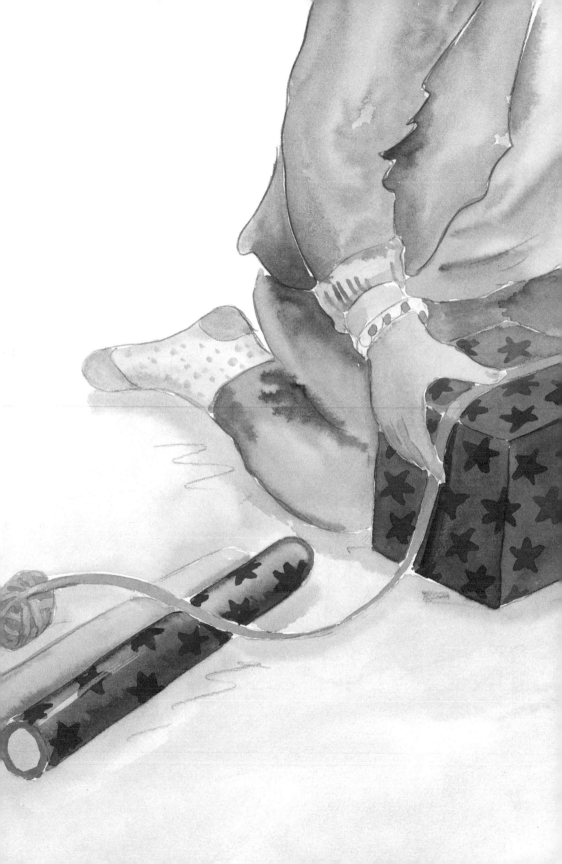

I can help wrap presents.

I can make holiday cards.

I can decorate the tree.

I can make Christmas music.

I can even wait
for Santa Claus.

Oops!
I forgot there's something
else I can do.

I can try the
Christmas cookies!